Neither Dead Nor Alive

Neither Dead Nor Alive

Jack Hastie

Cover design by Mandy Sinclair
www.mandysinclair.com

Matador
9 Priory Business Park
Kibworth Beauchamp
Leicestershire LE8 0RX, UK
Tel: (+44) 116 279 2299
Fax: (+44) 116 279 2277
Email: books@troubador.co.uk
Web: www.troubador.co.uk/matador

ISBN 978 1783065 059

British Library Cataloguing in Publication Data.
A catalogue record for this book is available from the British Library.

Typeset in Bembo by Troubador Publishing Ltd
Printed and bound in the UK by TJ International, Padstow, Cornwall

Matador is an imprint of Troubador Publishing Ltd

This book is dedicated to Amber, Erin, Mark and Courtney
The author's grandchildren

Chapter 1

THE SLEEPING DINOSAUR

That's it again.

I sit up in bed so I can hear better.

Each time it starts it's scarier than before. Where's it coming from? How near is it? At first it was just a noise. Now I swear I can feel it. It makes the windows rattle and it seems to be getting closer.

The thing is this place is dead quiet; not like when we lived in Paisley. There's not another house in sight.

Here it comes again.

It's a hoarse, throaty noise; something between a growl and a groan, only all muffled up.

I think I must be sweating because when I reach for my watch the steel bracelet feels greasy between my fingers.

It's four in the morning. Starting to get light already.

No use wakening Mum. If she didn't hear it last time she won't now… and I don't want her dragging me off to the doctor and telling him, "the boy's disturbed." It's freaky. I'm nearly thirteen and I don't get to be taken seriously.

Could I be dreaming?

Just to make sure I get up and open the window. There's just enough light outside for me to see the outline of the moor. There's a kind of rocky hillock out there. That might be where it's coming from.

Now I know I'm sweating. I can feel the chill prickle my skin.

There's not a sound now. It's weird. When you TRY to listen you don't hear a thing.

Might as well go back to bed.

****

Morning.

I don't know any kids round here – except Mark, that is – because we only moved in at the start of the school holidays. So I haven't been to school here yet.

We're pretty isolated. Nearest place is Benderloch. That's about half an hour's walk away. Need to get Dad to send my bike up. On the way there's a couple of old farm houses and a new caravan site. It's cool. They've got karting and diving and a sandy beach. Now the holidays have started there'll probably be some guys my age around, but not so far.

Across the road, among the trees, there's a castle on a hill. Mark says it's called the Black Castle and it's got a ghost – a white lady.

In the other direction there's the place where Mark lives. He's not been here long either, so we sort of team up – sometimes.

"What do you do around here?" I ask him.

"Sometimes go up to Benderloch. It's pretty dead, though. There's a cafe with some arcade games."

Bo-ring.

Mark's a bit of a plonker. Chews gum with his mouth open so you can see it at the back of his teeth. I told him about the noise – bad mistake. He laughed his head off – that's how I first noticed the gum. Mind you, I wasn't too sure about it – the noise, I mean – myself, at that time. Mark said I must have imagined it. But not after last night.

Today I go down the road to Mark's, kicking stones and dreaming I'm playing at Hampden.

Mark's place is brill. His back garden goes right down to the shore of the loch – that's Loch Creran – and there's a burn runs down the middle and flows into a bay. The loch's usually quite calm because it's almost landlocked and you can see big blue mountains on the other side.

Mark's in his garden.

"Hi, Mark."

"Hi, Duracell."

"Steve," I correct him. OK; so I've got sort of slightly reddish hair.

"Want to come round to my place?"

"Right."

Mark has a ball, so we kick it between us up the track. I'm St Mirren. He's Barcelona. He says he's always supported them.

"Thought we could take a look at that hilly sort of thing round our back."

"Why?"

"Well, you know the noise I've been hearing…"

Mark snorts. "That'll be right."

"Well I think it's coming from the hill."

He traps the ball and looks dead serious. "Maybe it's really a dinosaur that sleeps all day, but sometimes it wakens up and growls. Maybe we'll find its eyes and its ears. Come on."

He races ahead up the track with the ball under his arm.

"Mark," I shout after him, "no kidding. This isn't a game."

Then I wonder – could it be a sleeping dinosaur?

****

We're on the hill thing.

It's not really a hill. Just a jumble of rocks and boulders

with heather and bracken growing out of them. And it's definitely not a dinosaur. No eyes, no ears. Mark says he's found its mouth, but he's kidding – it's just the way the rocks look.

"See these big flat stones?" he says. "That's its lips. They're fossilised."

"That's just rocks."

"No they're not. They're too smooth. Besides, they fit together."

It's my turn to laugh. But I don't laugh for long.

For suddenly it's there, right below our feet – that growling, moaning noise; all muffled and smothered.

"Mark," I yell, "It's right under us."

He screws up his face. "What're you on about?"

"The noise, Mark. Can't you feel it? Like something ginormous is roaring about in the earth."

"Come off it." He bounces the ball casually off one of the big flat stones and catches it neatly.

Then the noise stops.

Mark is bouncing the ball off differently-shaped stones; so he has to leap about to catch it as it comes back.

I feel my heart thumping.

"Didn't you hear it?"

"Hear what?"

"The noise; the flaming noise, you dork."

"You really think you heard a noise?" He looks puzzled.

"Didn't you? A big booming noise. You've got to have heard it."

He shakes his head. "See you, Steve. You're a nutter."

****

Met another kid today, Fiona. Her dad drove round to see Mum. It seems they knew each other in the old days.

Played together as kids. Funny; I thought Mum had always lived in Paisley.

Mum introduces us. "Steve, this is Fiona. Fiona, Steve. Fiona's at the school in Oban; you'll be going to school in August. You might be in the same class."

Then we're left alone. A bit awkward. Fiona's got big brown eyes and a long black ponytail. She's got this irritating habit of twirling it round her finger. And can she ask questions!

"How long've you been here?"

"Bout a week."

"Where did you stay before?"

"Paisley; near Glasgow airport."

"Why'd you move?"

"My mum and dad split up. Mum's got a job in Oban."

"My dad works there too. He's head librarian. We've always lived here."

I think *that's why she speaks funny; sort of singy-songy*. But I don't say that. Instead I say, "Want to come round the back? There's this freaky heap of rocks. Mark says it's a dead dinosaur."

I decide not to tell her about the noise.

"Who's Mark?"

"Mark Telfer. Stays down by the loch."

"Him. He's a twit. He's not been here long, either. Thinks he knows everything about the place. I've lived here all my life." She twirls her ponytail indignantly.

Now we're near the hill thing and I have this funny feeling – what if the noise comes back again? I won't let her know, I decide. I don't want to be laughed at by a girl.

We pick around among the stones for a bit.

"Not a dead dinosaur," she announces. "Know what I think?"

"It's just a pile of rocks."

"It's a prehistoric tomb."

"A what?"

"A tomb. Look." She points to the big flat stones Mark called the dinosaur's lips.

"That's the way in."

"You can't get in there."

"Not now. It's all collapsed. But long ago… I'll ask my dad." There's a shout from the house; "Fiona, time to go."

Her dad goes back inside.

We're halfway across the garden when it starts again, louder than ever, like a huge buried beast bellowing – and now the ground is shaking and shuddering under our feet.

I forget that I'm not going to let her know I hear it and I freeze like I'm seeing a ghost, but it doesn't matter.

For a long second we stare at each other and then, without a word, we both turn and race for the house.

Chapter 2

SECRETS OF THE RED BOOK

Fiona comes round a lot these days.

Her dad drops her off. Think he's glad of an excuse to see my mum.

Fiona tells me she's trying to find out about the dead dinosaur. That noise really scared her and she reckons there should be something about it in her dad's library. She goes there with him and looks up old books and maps and things the ordinary guys don't get to see.

One day she changes the subject.

"Do you love your mum?" she asks.

That's uncool. I mean, what am I supposed to say?

What I do say is, "It's the Champions League tonight. Highlights are on the box. Mum says I can stay up and watch them."

"I wish I still had MY mum," she says. Her eyes are big and glistening, like she's going to cry.

"Hold on," I say. "I need to see about something."

I go to the toilet. I don't need to really, but I can't stand it when girls get soppy.

When I come back she's OK.

She tells me about Oban and I tell her about Paisley. We talk about records and stuff. She says there's sometimes a disco in Connel. That's where me and Mum got off the train the day we came here.

But whatever we're talking about she always comes back

to the dead dinosaur. I'm not much bothered about it now. Haven't heard the thing for days. Maybe it's gone really dead.

Fiona's fascinated with it, but she hasn't found out anything about it so far.

Today's different, though.

Me and Mark are round the back, kicking a ball about, when she appears with this book. It's got brown covers and the pages are yellowish.

Fiona opens it at the first page. I'm looking over her shoulder. It says:

THE RED BOOK OF CLANRANALD.

or

THE CHRONICLES OF THE HIGHLANDS FROM THE EARLIEST TIMES TO THE COMING OF CHRISTIANITY.

Translated by
Rev. Archibald Campbell, BD
Minister in the parish of Benderloch.

Then there's these letters:

MDCCC LXXIV

Fiona says that's the date and it's a hundred years old.

I say, "Cool," just to please her.

She tells us it's a copy of another book that's as old as the tomb Mark said was a dead dinosaur.

"Where did you nick it?" asks Mark.

"I BORROWED it," she says, "from the special collection in Dad's library."

"Cool," I say again. What I really think is *pure brill; a book as old as a dinosaur. Just what I need for the holidays.*

"There's a story in it," she explains, "about the Appin Cattle Raid."

"That's Appin over there," interrupts Mark. He jerks his thumb across the loch.

Fiona's got him taped. He thinks he knows all about the place. But he must have got it right this time, because she nods and starts reading:

"In those days a Benderloch chief called Fergus Snake-eye drove off the far-famed White Bull of Appin and stole a golden cauldron from Finn the Red. He forded Loch Creran with them and hid them near his village. The bull was sacred to The Morrigan, but she was angry with Finn because he had not sacrificed it to her that midsummer as he had promised."

"What's The Morrigan?" I ask.

She has to think for a moment.

"She's an old hag..." she begins.

"Like Mrs Campbell in the cafe in Benderloch." Mark guffaws at his joke so I can see the pink chewing gum on his back teeth.

"So she's still alive?" I ask.

"No, well... She's a... she was the goddess of battles. She used to appear as an old woman with only one eye. She often had a raven perched on her shoulder and an adder coiled round one wrist."

"Load of mince," snorts Mark.

"Why did Finn have to sacrifice the bull?" I ask.

"Santa Claus had a famous reindeer called Rudolf," interrupts Mark. "Rudolf had a red nose. One day an angel stole Rudolf..."

Fiona snaps her book shut. "If you're going to take the mickey," she screams.

"Go on," I say. "Belt up, Mark."

But she's really mad. She's blushing and she looks as if she might be going to cry again.

I don't know what to do. Mark's going on about a wise man wanting a red-nosed reindeer in his Christmas stocking. I feel like punching him but I don't want him to think I believe her cheesy story.

So she stomps off. Phones Daddy to come and pick her up.

When she's gone I pretend to laugh with Mark about her crazy book – but I'm not sure.

A couple of days later I'm talking to Mrs. Naysmith. Mum has her in to clean the house once a week, because she's out at work. Mrs. Naysmith tells me she does cleaning at the Black Castle.

"Ever see the ghost?" I ask. "Mark Telfer says it's haunted by a white lady."

"Not myself," she says. "But there's rumours about it."

"Go on."

"You wouldn't believe me."

"Yes, I would."

"Your mother will be giving me into trouble for filling your head with nonsense."

"I won't tell her."

"Well… folk say she walks in the round room, up in the turret, with her black raven on her shoulder and her white snake round her arm. And them that see her, something bad will happen to them before the year is out."

"Do you know anybody who's seen her?"

She nods.

"What happened to them?"

She shakes her head. "I must be getting on with my work. But if you should be seeing the white lady, don't you go looking her in the eye."

She switches on the Hoover, so we can't talk any more for the noise.

I wonder *is she winding me up?*

The next day Fiona rings me. "Do you want to hear the rest of the story, or not?"

"Sure."

"Is Mark there?"

"No."

"If he comes round you won't let him in."

"OK."

Her dad drops her off. She's got the book with her again.

I kind of apologize. Start to explain that I was just going to punch Mark when she dashed off… but she cuts me short.

"You remember about Finn the Red, the Appin chief who owned the white bull?"

I nod.

"And The Morrigan, the goddess of battles?"

"Uh-uh." I could tell her another story about The Morrigan now, but I reckon it's better just to listen.

"You wanted to know why Finn had to sacrifice the bull to her."

"Uh-uh."

Fiona opens her book and begins to read:

"Finn was a great chief but he didn't have a son to succeed him, although he had five daughters. So he prayed to The Morrigan not to let his line die out. She promised one of his wives would give him a son, but in return he would have to sacrifice the most valuable animal in all his herds when the boy reached his twelfth birthday. Finn swore that he would do this.

"A boy was born and was named Aidan. On the same day one of Finn's cows gave birth to a pure white bull calf. This was taken to be an omen because in those days all the cattle in the land were black. Some said it was unlucky and

11

should be killed at once. But, because it had been born on the same day as his son, Finn ordered it to be spared.

"It grew up to be the strongest and fiercest bull in the land and many neighbouring chiefs offered Finn great wealth in bronze and gold and slaves if he would give it to them. But Finn always said it was his son's lucky bull and refused to part with it.

At last Fergus Snake-eye gave Finn a cauldron of pure gold. Finn claimed it was a gift, but Fergus insisted that it was meant to be in exchange for the bull.

"A few weeks later, at midsummer, Aidan celebrated his twelfth birthday. The Morrigan appeared, first as a raven, then as an adder to remind Finn of the promise he had made all those years before – but he refused to sacrifice the bull to her. Then Fergus stole it along with the cauldron and the sacred duty of sacrifice fell upon him."

"Where did Fergus hide the bull and the cauldron?" I ask.

"It doesn't say. At least I can't find it, but I haven't read the whole book yet."

"So it's just a story," I say. "The Morri-whatsit's like Athene in the Trojan War. She got things sacrificed to her."

It's my turn to show off now. In primary seven we did a project on the Trojan War.

Fiona just twirls her ponytail.

I feed her the question again.

"This Morr-woman's just like the Greek gods, then?"

She doesn't answer me. Instead she points to the dead dinosaur.

"That hill's got a name," she announces. "Dad showed me on an old map. It's called, "Cnoc an Oir."

"Knock on what?"

"It's Gaelic," she says. "It means Hill of Gold."

Chapter 3

THE LAND OF THE OLD

Mark's gone to Oban with his folks for the day, so I think I'll go into Benderloch. Dad's not sent my bike on yet, so I'll have to walk.

I decide to take a short cut across the fields. There's clumps of bracken and yellow broom all over the place, and lots of rocks and trees and sourish blaeberries. I pick a few as I go along. There's sheep too – dirty white with black faces.

After a while I think there's more trees than there should be and I'm just beginning to wonder if I'm off course when I see these cows. They're too small, about the size of a Shetland pony. They've got these long twisty horns, like Highland cattle, but they're black. In these fields there should be sheep.

I'm not bothered. But the woods are getting thicker and tangled until I'm sure this isn't the way I've come before. Besides, there ought to be some farm buildings on the right – it's called Achnasomething – but I can't see them.

By now I'm sure I'm off the track. There's a big rock in the middle of the woods here and I climb up to the top to get a view.

It's freaky. I should be able to see the caravan site from here, but it's all trees and bushes. What's really weird is I'm not lost at all. I'm in the right place. Dead ahead's a slab of cliff on the hill beyond Benderloch, so I know I'm heading the right way. The Black Castle should be around here somewhere, but I can't see it for the trees.

Then I wonder – am I dreaming? Things don't go right for you in dreams – you get lost and can't find places, and that's what's happening just now. I start to climb down the boulder. Then my foot slips. I bang my shin against the rock and fall off. I land on my hip on a sharp stone and it's sore.

The pain feels real enough.

This gives me an idea how to check if I am in a dream. If I charge straight into the woods I'll get so banged up with branches and scratched with brambles that I'll waken up. I once dreamed I was falling off a cliff. Then I wakened. I'd fallen out of bed. I'm really chuffed with this idea; so I charge straight into the densest thickets and claw my way through branches thick with thorns. The backs of my hands get scratched by brambles and my jeans get torn.

But I don't waken up.

Instead I break through into a kind of clearing. Dead ahead of me is the cliff on the Benderloch hill; so this is where the Black Castle should be, only it's not there. Instead the clearing's got a kind of hedge all round it – not a growing hedge, but thorny stuff all pulled together on top of a bank. There's a gap in the hedge, like a gate, and I'm looking straight through it.

Inside the hedge I see – at first I'm not sure what they are. I screw up my eyes and shade them from the sun with my hand, but that doesn't make it any clearer.

I decide they must be houses. They're round, made of big stones that fit into each other like a dry stone dyke. They've got pointed roofs covered with heather like a thatch.

There's about a dozen of these huts arranged in a circle just inside the thorny hedge. Some have got smoke coming out of the top, like they're on fire. Right in the middle there's a bigger hut that's long and squarish. There's kids and hens and dogs playing around.

I decide I don't want them to see me. So I back into some

dense bracken. I've got this idea that something's going to happen, so I squat down. I'm going to wait and see.

A group of men come out of the big hut. They're weird. They've all got their trousers tucked into their boots and they've got big droopy moustaches. They haven't got beards, but they've got really long hair and it's tied up in a kind of knot at the back, like a ponytail.

Suddenly I'm thinking about Fiona. She'd freak out if she saw this. The geek would probably rush off and look it up in her daddy's library. "There's a book as old as a dinosaur..."

I'm shattered out of thinking about her because there's this big riot and they're all shouting and freaking in some foreign language. The noise they're making is weird, but what's weirder is – I can understand what they're saying.

"Fergus!" they're shouting. "Space for Fergus. Make way for the king."

Now I notice for the first time there's an animal tethered to a post in front of the big hut. At first I think it must be a sheep. Then I see its horns. It's a goat.

I'm riveted by this, now.

The other guys are still shouting, "Fergus. Fergus. Step forth Fergus. Satisfy the Great One. Save us from evil."

This humungous great hairy bloke comes out of the biggest hut. I think he must be special, cos he's wearing a cloak over his shirt and he's got a yellow collar like twisted wire round his neck. Then he turns and looks straight at me through the gap in the hedge. For a second I think maybe he's seen me and I should run. But I can't move.

At least, one of his eyes is looking at me. The other's staring somewhere else; the Appin hills, maybe. But his good eye makes up for it. It's glaring like a light bulb.

Fergus hasn't seen me. At least – if he has – he doesn't let on.

He unties the goat's tether from the post and takes the animal on to a big flat stone I hadn't noticed before. He pulls a big cup, not a teacup – more like the Scottish Cup – from some place in his cloak and sets it on the flat stone.

Then suddenly he starts to chant, "The Morrigan. The Morrigan," softly at first. Then louder and louder.

The others take up the shout, "The Morrigan. The Morrigan."

What happens next is too quick to see. Fergus slides his hand under his shirt, whips out a knife that shines like fire and cuts the goat's throat. Blood belches and Fergus catches it in the big cup. The goat falls on its knees and its head almost topples off.

Fergus is still screaming, "The Morrigan."

The goat's blood is spurting out all over his face, soaking his moustache.

I'm gonna be sick. I retch a couple of times. I just want to get away. I turn and run, right through leaves and branches. I must be making a heck of a noise, but I keep going.

Then I'm down; tripped on a root. I shut my eyes and lie there. But they don't come after me.

After I don't know how long I open my eyes. It's all quiet, so I pick myself up and thread my way through the bushes. I remember now that I'm lost and I don't know whether I'll be able to get back home, especially as it's starting to get dark.

My head's down and I'm sort of staggering on. Then I bump into something. It's a wire fence. On the other side of it's a road – the road I was on. Then I see three sheep, white with black faces.

Which way home, then? I glance at the Appin hills and the Benderloch cliff – grey in the dusk – climb the fence and turn right up the road.

Chapter 4

IT'S GOT TO BE YOU

I'm picking a scab. There's a tear in my jeans. That's how I know I was there. I didn't think Mark 'n' Fiona'd believe me, but I told them all the same. Mark is inspecting the tear like an expert.

"Barbed wire fence," he announces.

I shrug. I'm looking at the backs of my hands – all scratched.

Mark nods at the dead dinosaur. "Big bramble patch over there. Good try, Duracell."

He laughs and I see he has changed the colour of his chewing gum.

Fiona isn't laughing. She's got the old book in her hands. She tells us we have to pay attention.

She begins to read. Mark puts on his Walkman and pretends not to listen.

"Finn the Red came over from Appin with his young son Aidan to recover the bull and the cauldron. But Fergus had bribed Gawawl Grimtooth, king of the Firbogs, to hide them in an underground tomb. His reward was to be the possession of the cauldron for himself."

"What's a Firbog?" I interrupt.

"They're sort of like gnomes. They live under the earth."

"I know." Mark takes his headphones off. "They're really called gommies. We've got one in the garden. It's red. But it's got a crack in it."

Fiona twirls her ponytail impatiently.

I say, "Belt up. I don't know about all this old stuff, but there's something scary going on and Fiona thinks the book can help us to find out about it."

She goes on, "Finn found the treasure, but Gawawl killed him and Aidan narrowly escaped with his life. Fergus Snake-eye knew that his life would never be safe as long as the boy was alive and, just three days later, he hunted him down with a pack of Elkhounds."

"What's Elkhounds?" asks Mark, though he's got the headphones back on.

"An elk was a huge deer, bigger than a horse," she explains. "The dogs were bred to kill them. They could tear wolves apart."

"Bet they didn't get him," says Mark.

"They did. They tore him to pieces, just outside the tomb, while Fergus Snake-eye looked on."

She turns back to the book: "However, Fergus also refused to sacrifice the white bull to The Morrigan. What was much worse, he tried to trick her – her, a goddess. He offered her a white billy goat in the hope that, because she's old and blind in one eye, she would not notice the deception.

"But The Morrigan has the eyes of a raven when she wishes to see and she was not deceived. She took the form of a great white adder and bit him to the bone so that he died in agony.

"So all the mortals perished – Finn and Fergus and young Aidan. But the vengeance of The Morrigan was not satisfied. She called up her raven and her adder as witnesses and she decreed that every year at midsummer all three would rise from the dead and re-enact their dooms afresh, each dying again – Finn at the hands of Gawawl, Aidan torn by the dogs and Fergus by the tooth of the snake – till the end of time."

"For ever and ever?" I whisper.

18

"Perhaps not." She turns the page. "It says here that Manannan, the god of the sea and the mist, persuaded The Morrigan that the punishment was too terrible – to be dead, yet never to be allowed to rest. So she relented and said that if one day someone of the clan of Finn would come and make the proper sacrifice, she would release Finn, Fergus and Aidan from the curse and they could all die at last and be at peace."

It's a good story. Mark has even put the Walkman away.

"Don't you see?" she asks me. "Fergus Snake-eye was the man you saw in the village and he sacrificed a white goat to The Morrigan."

Mark breaks open a new pack of spearmint. "Believe that and you'll believe anything."

I don't know what to think. I ask, "Then what happened to me yesterday?"

She closes the book. "I don't know. I think you must have somehow walked into the past, to the time of the Appin Raid. I don't know how or why... but you could hear the bellowing from inside that tomb. That must have been the ghost of the white bull. And now you've been able to walk right back into the past. You've seen Fergus Snake-eye in the flesh! You know what?"

"What?"

"*You* must be the one who will free them all from The Morrigan's curse."

"Dream on," I laugh. Mostly it's a funny ha-ha laugh, but I'm scared.

"You will have to go back into the past again, and find the bull and sacrifice it... "

I go ballistic. "That's crazy. I don't know how I got there – or how I got out again. And I'm not into sacrificing bulls. I am DEFINITELY not going back."

"... before it's too late," Fiona adds quietly. "Before poor Aidan has to die again."

19

Mark has stopped chewing.

"A man's gotta do… " he chimes in.

I turn on him. "Piss off!"

He gets up and walks away. "See you later, Superman."

I'm shaking.

Then I have this brill idea. "This frigging hero's meant to be a… a who?"

"Someone of the clan of Finn," she prompts.

"That lets me out," I shout. "I'm a Paisley Buddy."

It's crazy how proud I suddenly am to be a Buddy.

"If you're proud to be a Buddy clap your hands," I chant.

She cuts me short. "Your mum was born in Appin. She knew my dad when they were kids. It's got to be you."

"No way."

"What was your mum's maiden name?"

I know, but I'm not going to tell her!

Chapter 5

GAWAWL GRIMTOOTH

Mum's gone to Paisley today. Think she might be going to see my dad. She couldn't get a babysitter, so I've got the day to myself.

I'm to "be careful." What else can you do in this joint? Mark's away, too, and I don't fancy another lecture from that geek Fiona.

So what to do? It'll be boring, anyway.

Could go up to Benderloch. Play some arcade games in the cafe. Maybe meet some kids. Bound to be some around, now school's finished.

This time, though, I'll stick to the road – just in case.

So here I am; all right so far – plod, plod. I'm glancing around from side to side just to check. As I go along I stop and pick a few rasps or blaeberries. It's too early for the brambles.

At least I'm past Achnawhatsit, the place that disappeared last time.

A bit further on I hear this rustling noise in the heather, so I stop and have a look. A big dog is loping away across the moor. It's like an Alsatian except it's grey all over. I watch it for a bit until it disappears among some rocks.

Then I turn round.

I don't believe this.

I kick my left shin with my right foot. "Get real, Steve," I gasp. Achnawhatsit's not there. It's just bushes and trees. I hear a long howl from among the boulders and I realize that what I saw was a wolf.

My stomach turns over inside me.

Right! I have to get BACK – to today. Last time this happened I got back when I found the road again. This time, though, there's a problem. The road's disappeared. There's only a muddy track where it should be.

There's another problem, too. Something's coming up the track towards me, going towards our house.

I want to back into the bushes out of sight, but – trust my luck – just here there's no bushes, only low tufts of heather.

So I just stand here as if I'm brave or something.

Two horsemen are on the track. The first one's on this small black horse, more like a pony really, with a red bridle. He's a big guy, a bit like Fergus, but with OK eyes. He's got red hair, like flames, and a ponytail and a droopy red moustache. And he's wearing a twisty yellow collar, like Fergus.

The second rider's a kid about my age and he's got sandy hair, just like me. It's longer, of course, and it's done up in a ponytail too.

The big horseman stops. He looks down at me. His horse gets its head down and starts eating grass at the side of the track.

He's speaking in that funny language – and I'm understanding him.

"Are you of our clan?"

I shake my head.

He kind of shudders and walks the horse on slowly as if he doesn't really want to go any further.

The other horse with the kid on top comes up to me.

"What's your name?" the kid asks.

I feel my chest tighten and I can't get my breath, cos it's as if I'm looking at my own face, except for the ponytail at the back.

"Steve," I gasp.

"Steve," he repeats. He looks disappointed. "That's not a king's name. I am Aidan, son of Finn, son of Diarmid. Our clan is royal. There," he points to the big guy, "is my father, Finn, the king."

He moves his horse on.

I should go back and see if I can hit the proper road somewhere, but I can't. I have to go forward and follow the boy with my face.

The horses are getting ahead of me now. I break into a run. Then I stop. Maybe I'm not meant to catch up. But Aidan turns his horse and comes back.

"Do you want to ride?"

He gives me a hand to pull up on. Now I'm sitting behind him. I've never been on a horse before. It's really high up.

"We're going to get the bull," says the boy with my face. "My bull, born on the same day as I was. We've tried before, but I've never seen you here till today. Perhaps you can help us."

I think about Fiona and the old book. Should I warn the boy? What should I say to him?

"You're not one of Fergus' people?" he asks.

"No."

"Then why are you here? And why are you wearing these clothes? He half turns and points to the buttons on my jacket and shirt. I see his clothes don't have buttons.

"And that bracelet." He touches my watch strap. "I've never seen one like that."

"I'm new here," I say. The words come out in English, but he seems to understand.

"So you're not one of Fergus' people?"

"No," I say again. I'm honest this time. I remember the murder of the goat and all the blood and that glittering eye. "I hate Fergus."

He puts his heels to the horse. "Dad," he calls, "Steve'll help us."

It's hard to tell, with all the bushes and trees being different, but by looking at the Appin hills and the Benderloch cliff I reckon we must be back at about the place our cottage should be. It's not there, of course.

But the dead dinosaur is. It's not all overgrown with heather and bracken like today. It's a mound of freshly dug earth with a circle of ginormous stones round its base like a kerb.

From inside it comes that noise – the sound of a bull tethered in the dark, mad with anger and fear.

Finn dismounts and hands the reins to Aidan.

"The voice of the bull," he says. "And here must our gold be also."

He draws a long sword which I think is weird because it's broader just behind the tip than at the handle and it gleams like fire in the sunshine. He stalks slowly towards the entrance of the mound. Now I see what Mark thought were the dinosaur's lips – big stone slabs, upright like a gateway.

Aidan and I slide off our horse and wait.

Aidan is holding the reins. He hands me a blade. It's not real metal. It looks a bit like gold, but it's quite tinny.

Finn inches forward.

At first I think nobody's guarding the bull.

Then there's a shadowy thing between the big stones at the entrance. First this hairy hand appears, with the fingers clasping and unclasping round the edges of the stones. Then a face like a monkey, only it's got these gross teeth. They're jutting out of its jaws and one of them's sticking out sideways like a broken bone.

For a few seconds the face stays there, peering out from under the stones. I notice it's got slavers drooling from its big tooth. That makes me want to be sick. And there's a stink off it like rotten cabbage.

Finn shouts, "Gawawl, come out in peace. Between us there need be no quarrel."

But it comes right at us across the heather like it's in megadrive.

Finn slashes at it with his sword, but it knocks the blade out of his hand and jumps on him. I see the gross teeth meet round his neck. Then I hear a crunch, like a dog cracking a bone.

Aidan shouts, "Dad," and runs forward with this wee knife he has. But the beast knocks him sideways with its arm and he falls across the track. I run forward to pull him clear, but the thing's almost on top of us.

I reckon it's curtains, whatever Fiona's book says, but I throw up my hand – as if that would keep the beast off.

Funny thing is, it does.

It stops.

I'm looking right up into this stinking mouth, but it doesn't come for me. It's got these bloodshot eyes and it's blinking them wide. I swear it's afraid.

Aidan hustles me towards some bushes.

Just in time. The thing with the teeth is clawing at me. But it's not looking me in the face. It turns its head away as it comes.

Then Aidan grabs me again.

He dives me right into the undergrowth like he's done this sort of thing before.

We're in among some hawthorns. They're pretty dense, but there's tunnels under them you can crawl through and we scramble along them for a bit.

Then we crouch down. I can hear the thing strutting and swaggering up and down, looking for us. I'm dead sure it'll hear my breathing, but Aidan whispers, "Gawawl won't find us here."

So I'm brave enough to look out. I can see it through the

leaves. It doesn't look all that tall, but it's got these humungous great arms and animal skins instead of proper clothes.

Aidan grips my elbow, "Come."

He crawls along one of these tunnels and I follow him.

After a while Gawawl's snortings and ravings get quieter until I can't hear them at all.

We're out of the hawthorns now, into something thorny like brambles. So it's more difficult to crawl through them.

Aidan says, "We're safe now," and stands up.

I feel blood trickling down my forehead from the thorns. I put up my hand to wipe it away and I get mud in my eye.

I can't see for a second or two.

Then my eyes clear and I stand up beside him.

There's a voice in my ear. "How the heck did you get here?"

I am looking into the eyes of Mark Telfer.

Chapter 6

COLD IRON

I'm on the phone to Fiona. I'm gibbering. "I'm not going out of the house."

"Get real," she says.

"This is for real. If that happens again I'm finished."

"It won't happen again, at least not the way it did."

"How d'you know? It just happens."

"It doesn't JUST happen. I know HOW it happens."

Yuck! I can see her smirk all the way down the telephone line.

"I've found another book. I'll bring it round. Dad'll drop me off. You'll be in, won't you?"

She's taking the mickey now.

And she's got another lousy old book. That's all I need.

I jump when the door bell rings. I haven't heard her dad's car, so I check at the window in case it's Gawawl.

It's Mark.

I'm even glad to see him, so I let him in.

He's convinced I'm a complete nutter since he found me crawling around on my hands and knees in a bramble patch.

"Still looking for gommies?" he laughs, showing off his latest brand of gum.

Before I can think of what to say the bell goes again. This time it's Fiona. Her dad's dropped her off and before I can get to the door he's reversing back down the drive. Doesn't he realise what could happen to her?

I let her in and it's clear she's all wound up. She's got this book in her hand – a different book this time – and a long parcel wrapped up in brown paper.

But she doesn't open it – the book or the parcel.

Instead she asks a stupid question: "Yesterday, before you met Finn and Aidan, did you eat anything?"

"What's that got to do with it?"

"What did you eat?"

"Nothing."

"Pick any berries?"

"A few rasps. Maybe some blaeberries."

She's twirling her ponytail like a windmill and she's almost dancing with excitement.

"Time before?"

"Can' t remember."

"You might have picked some blaeberries?"

"Could've done."

She sits down on the settee and opens the book on her knee. I can see she's taking her time – deliberately.

"An Account of a Journey Through the Countie of Argyll, by James McPhee Esq." she reads. "He wrote this two hundred years ago."

"Get on with it then."

She turns to where she's put in a bit of paper to mark the place. "Superstitions abound among the inhabitants. Belief in the Firbog, a malevolent kind of gnome, which – being earthbound – cannot cross running water, is almost universal.

"In the districts of Appin and Benderloch it is widely believed that, for a few days after midsummer, the unwary traveller..."

She gets too excited to go on reading. She says, "It goes on and on, but what it really means is that people wander into the past – the Land of the Old – and sometimes they don't come back."

Mark's stopped chewing. He's listening with his mouth open.

"How?" I ask.

"It says there's a blaeberry... hold on a sec..."

She finds her place in the book. "which is said to grow only in these parts and whose freshly picked fruit, in consequence of an ancient charm, is believed to confer the ability – or some say the necessity – to travel into the past.

"It may be supposed that the juice of these berries, when freshly picked, contains a property which may induce delusions in the minds of the superstitious."

She adds, "You picked blaeberries, didn't you?"

"Maybe." I give her my best 'unimpressed' look.

"Both times?"

"Look, the book says 'delusions'."

Mark comes to life. "Like doing drugs." He starts chewing again. For him the spell is broken. "Duracell's high on something. Bad trip, was it?"

I ignore him. I'm shouting at Fiona, "Gawawl and the rest are real. I had real scabs and scratches... and the bellowing bull; we both heard that."

"I didn't," says Mark.

Fiona ignores him too. "Mark's an incomer," she tells me.

"So am I," I remind her. "I'm a Paisley Buddy."

"Are you really? I mean really, really?"

I change the subject. "What was that about a charm?"

"I don't know yet. I'll have to look through the Red Book again. But, you know, if The Morrigan prophesied that someone of the race of Finn would one day stop the whole terrible business, she must have made a way of getting him into the scene."

"Then how did I get back to today?"

"I don't know that either. Maybe the effect just wears off."

"So, if you're right, we know how I got into the past. That makes one thing sure."

"What?"

"I won't be making the same mistake again."

"You jerk."

I go ballistic. "You've not seen that Gawawl thing – he's gross – or Fergus with the eye. All right for you. You just sit here nice and cosy and Daddy drives you around in his car... "

"Shut up," she interrupts. "Now listen to this."

She opens the book at another place she's marked.

"Get a load of this. `In the midst of so many imagined dangers from the unseen world, the sturdy peasant takes courage from the fact that iron is held to be a charm against almost all evil.

`Reck you not the warlock, the kelpie or the troll
   For iron – cold iron – is master of them all`."

"So what's the big deal?"

"You said that Gawawl seemed afraid of you. You said he turned his face away. What were you doing at that moment?"

"I dunno. Put my arm up..." I raise my left hand.

"What's that made of?" she points.

My steel watch bracelet is glinting on my wrist.

"What's the score then?" I ask. "It's only a watch."

"Fergus and Finn and all the rest of them lived in the Bronze Age," she explains. "Those swords and knives you saw were made of bronze. The only iron they knew came from the stars."

"How the stars?"

"Meteors. Shooting stars. Sometimes a shooting star falls to the ground and people find iron. In the Bronze Age, before blacksmiths knew how to make iron in furnaces they thought it came from the gods. And it's a lot harder than bronze, so they were scared of it."

"All of them. Even Gawawl?"

"All of them except maybe The Morrigan. Something else – I know about your mum."

I've been waiting for this.

"Her name's Mrs. Hamilton. She used to live in Paisley," I say, but I know it's hopeless.

"My dad knew her when they were kids. She lived over there in Appin. Her name was Morag McAlpine." She stops as if there's no answer to that.

"So what?"

"McAlpine," she repeats.

"So?"

"Didn't your mum ever tell you about the McAlpines?"

"I just heard the name."

Fiona's staring straight ahead now, not looking at Mark or me. It's as if she's reading from a book we can't see.

"The McAlpines are descended from Kenneth, son of Alpine, the first king of all Scotland. He was the thirtieth successor of Fergus Mor, who drove the garrisons left by the Romans out of our country, and Fergus was the fortieth in direct line from Cormac, whose mother was the eldest daughter of Finn the Red. Now after Aidan died Cormac was the true heir so... "

"OK, skip the history lesson," I cut her short.

"You are a McAlpine. You are of the race of Finn."

"You don't know that. You're just making it up."

"My dad told me. My mum was a McAlpine too."

I look at Mark. I'm hoping he'll say something really cheesy that will break the spell. But he's spooked by all this too. I'm wondering if he's swallowed his gum.

Fiona's talking again. "You've got to go back and stop Aidan from being torn to pieces again by the dogs. You saw

Gawawl kill Finn yesterday. The Red Book says Aidan was killed three days later. That means you've got just two days left."

She's tearing open her parcel. "Look."

I don't believe this. She's giving me a blade a foot long with a staghorn handle.

"Take this dirk," she says. "It's forged of iron. So long as you don't panic it will give you protection over everything in the Land of the Old – except The Morrigan herself."

I don't move.

"Remember; Aidan saved your life yesterday. He has to die every midsummer for ever and ever."

I take the blade.

I mumble something about not knowing where to go or what to do in the Land of the Old.

"Don't worry about that," she says. "I'm coming with you."

Chapter 7

BACK TO BEING A BUDDY

I'm lying awake in bed. Thinking. It's got to be today or tomorrow. Mum got home late last night. I was sleeping. Fiona's still got the dirk. I'm not chickening out. But I've no place to hide it and if she's coming too she might as well hold on to it.

I'm all psyched up. It's like I've got a secret weapon, like a laser gun. I mean. if my watch strap could sort out old Gawawl what'll a real Highland dirk do?

I'm thinking over in my head how I'll play it. Gawawl will come slavering at me. Fiona will be behind me. I'll say "Stand back, traitor." Then he'll charge. I'll let him come on a bit. Then I'll draw the dirk. I'll say something like, "Thus far and no further" and he'll scuffle to a stop. Then I'll... well, I'll have to work that bit out later. Mum's just come into my room.

"Morning, Stevey," she says.

I hate 'Stevey'. Rather be called 'Duracell.'

"Time to get up. We're going back to Paisley today." My stomach drops down into my guts.

She goes on, "Isn't that great? You'll see all your pals again and Dad'll be there ..." She's bright and smiling like I haven't seen her for ages, but she soon tails off. Maybe she's guessed from my face I'm not exactly over the moon.

"Dad'll take you to see St Mirren again... and," – I guess she's pretty desperate now – "the planes at the airport."

My brain freezes.

I can't tell her.

"You can invite Mark down to stay with us during the holidays – or at weekends."

I get out of bed, brush my teeth.

"Mum."

"Yes, Stevey."

"Could we leave it till tomorrow?"

"No way." I hear a smile singing in her voice. "We're all back together again for always and always and always." She rushes into the bathroom and hugs me.

I wonder... does Mark have to put up with this sort of thing? Somehow I don't think so.

I eat my breakfast. We've a taxi booked to take us to Benderloch; then the bus to Connel; then the train. We've not got much luggage. It's all been so quick. Mum and Dad are getting back together and it's got to be today. The luggage can come on later. Dad never got round to sending my bike up, anyway.

I'm thrilled about Dad and Mum. My dad's great. If he was coming up here I'd be over the moon. We could go swimming again and I reckon he'd fancy a go at the karting at the caravan site. But he's got his job in Paisley; so we've got to go there.

****

We're on the train now. There's a couple of hours before we get to Glasgow. Then we change stations for Paisley. So I've got time to think.

I've got to get back to the Bronze Age by tomorrow, before Aidan is killed again. So I've got to get back to Benderloch today.

I'm working out how to do that. This train goes to Queen

Street station in Glasgow. Then we get a minibus that takes us to Central station. So I can give Mum the slip in Queen Street and get a train back here.

I've no dosh for a ticket, but you don't need one to get on and I can always hide in the toilet when the inspectors come round.

Right; that's what I'll do.

Then Mum drops her bombshell. "Dad's going to meet us at Queen Street."

I'm pure stunned. I look out the window so she can't see my face. That's my plan shredded. If Dad meets us at the station I'm trapped. I could tell him everything, of course. Could tell Mum, just now, on the train. But who'd believe me? Suddenly I know I've gotta get off this train.

We're slowing down. I've been so busy trying to figure things out I hadn't noticed. We stop at a station; Loch Awe. One or two people get on and we're away again. Now I know what I've got to do. I'll get off at the next station and take a train back.

I ask Mum: "What's the next stop?"

"Dalmally," she says. "Bout a quarter of an hour."

****

Here I am at Dalmally. As soon as the train started slowing down I got up to go to the toilet. Nipped off when we stopped. I suppose I got a bit lucky cos Mum was sitting on the other side of the train, so she didn't see me.

But now there's another hitch. As soon's the train's away I ask this man: "When's the next train back to Connel?"

"Fourteen fifty-eight," he says.

"Eh?"

"Three o'clock; you've a long wait."

I look at my watch. It's just a quarter past one. Can't hang around here for two hours. Sooner or later Mum's gonna miss me and then she'll raise the alarm.

I wander out of the station and down to the main road. There's a sign. It says 'Oban' one way and 'Crianlarich' the other. I go the Oban way. Connel's just before Oban, but it's too far to walk.

There might be a bus, but I've no money and it's starting to rain. Besides I've got to get out of here before the police start looking for me. I wonder about hitching a lift. I've not done that before, but I know you wave your thumb and cars and stuff stop and give you a ride.

I decide to give it a try but there's not much traffic on the road and nobody wants to stop. I keep going for about an hour and I'm just about ready to pack it in and settle for the long walk when this GTi screams past.

Suddenly there's a screech of brakes and it stops ahead of me. The driver's window's right down and some group's belting out on the stereo. I'm running now – just in case he revs away. But he doesn't. It's a well smart car; personalised number plates, alloy wheels, back spoiler; the lot.

The passenger door opens and a woman gets out. She's got a YSL T-shirt, Armani jeans – I can see the label – and Nike trainers.

"Where do you want to go?"

"Benderloch."

"Darren," she turns to the driver. "Benderloch. Ever heard of it?"

Darren's on his mobile. He switches it off and puts his head out the window. He's got an earring and he's wearing shades even though it's raining.

"Take him as far as Connel, Vicki. And that's it."

"OK," says Vicki. "Climb in the back."

"And don't touch anything," growls Darren.

"You'll have to squeeze in beside the gear," says Vicki.

"Darren's a DJ. We're doing a gig in Oban tonight."

I'm stuck in the back of this hatchback. The seats are folded down and it's crammed with these decks and amps. And Darren's driving like he's in a rally.

"What's your game, wee man?" he asks.

Am I gonna tell him I've gotta get back to the Bronze Age? He answers for me,

"Frigged off with the old dears?"

"Yeah."

"Been there." He sounds a bit friendlier now. "Bought the T- shirt. So you think you're gonna hit the road?"

Vicki interrupts, "What's your name?"

"Steve."

"Do you know anybody in Benderloch, Steve?"

"My mum's there." It's safe enough to say that cos she won't be at home.

"Thought you wanted away from her," says Darren.

"It's my dad."

"What's it with him?" asks Vicki.

"Don't want to go to stay with him."

"Why not?"

Then I blurt it all out; well, some of it. About being put on the train to Glasgow to meet my dad and not wanting to go back to Paisley. I don't tell them my mum was on the train with me and they're getting back together. I make it like Mum's still at Benderloch and I'm trying to get back to her.

"Your mum put you on the Glasgow train on your own?" asks Vicki.

"She asked the guard to look after me."

"What do you think, Darren?" she asks.

"Dump him at Connel. Let him find his own way back to Mummy."

"We can't just do that." She's thinking hard. "If we're going to take him to his mum, we'll take him all the way and make sure he gets there. Can't be all that far off our route. Tell you what – we'll phone her with the mobile."

"She's not in," I interrupt.

"How d'you know?" Darren sounds suspicious.

"Cos she works in Oban all day."

"Do you know her works number?" asks Vicki.

"No."

"Could you take us to where she works, then?"

"Never been there."

"Darren, we'll have to take him to the police."

"You off your trolley? With all that gear in the back?" She bites her lip.

"All right, then. We'll take him to his mum's house in Benderloch."

"That'll be shining bright."

"It's the least we can do.

"Were you born thick? Sooner or later that train guard's gonna report the kid missing. The Fuzz'll be all over the place from Dalmally to Benderloch and maybe even Oban. Look, we're nearly at Connel. We ditch him there and take the back road over the hill to Oban."

Her face sort of wrinkles. I can see she's not sure.

"I suppose... "

"Suppose nothing. We gotta get outa this before things start to go pear-shaped."

We're into houses now and there's a sign marked `Connel`. Darren slews the car round the steep corner that leads to the road to Benderloch. Then he turns into a side road and stops.

"Out," he snaps.

Vicki lets me out.

"That's your road, sunshine." He jerks his thumb backwards.

"Hold on, Darren." Vicki's rolled down her window and

she's fumbling with her purse. "You got any money, Steve? I'll just give him his bus fare to Benderloch."

"Give him nothing."

He crunches into gear and screeches away. His back wheels throw up a lot of wee stones into my face.

Chapter 8

ON THE RUN

I'm at Ledaig farm. I'm soaked. Had to walk from Connel. There's been a few cars but I didn't try to hitch. Couldn't take the chance the police might be looking for me – not after what Darren said.

I reckon I'm all right now. There's rocks and bushes on one side of the road, so I can dive in and hide if I have to. And just round the corner is Benderloch village and that's where Fiona's house is.

I'm just beginning to feel safe, but I'm still listening for the 'EEE-AAWW, EEE-AAWW, EEE-AAWW" of a police siren and I'm looking for blue flashing lights. Searching for me has got to be a big police emergency; so I don't notice this Vauxhall Astra purring along slowly, even though it's got police markings – not until it's too late.

I dive into a ditch. Maybe they haven't seen me. The car's cruising past. No; it's reversing right up to where I am. The front passenger door opens and a policewoman gets out.

"Steve," she calls.

I get my head down and don't breathe.

"Steve, you're not going to get into trouble."

Another door slams.

A man's voice asks, "Any sign of him?"

"I'm sure I saw him," she says. "must be somewhere over there." "Let's go see."

I can't help looking up and this policeman's coming

towards me, balancing from tussock to tussock among the muddy pools.

I leg it and he dives after me.

For a split second I think he's like a big black swan landing on a loch – all feet and arms flailing and splashing. He didn't see the soft mud and he's in over his knees.

That gives me the break I need. I'm into brambles and bracken and boulders and I'm half running, half crawling. I can hear them somewhere behind me and I think my heart's going to explode through my ribs.

There's a kind of tunnel in the bracken here and I double back along it. Can't keep this up much longer. Here's a hole under a big rock. It goes right underneath it, out of sight. I crawl under the rock.

I'm panting. Wish I didn't have to breathe so hard in case they hear me. But they're not close. In fact they're going the wrong way. I can hear them stomping and shouting and it's getting fainter.

Then the noise stops altogether. They must have given up.

But there's this other voice. "Stevey."

It's Mum.

"Stevey, please come out. We won't go back to Paisley if you don't want to. Please."

I wish I could tell her about Fiona and Aidan and all, but she wouldn't listen. I'd be grounded for weeks – and I've only got till tomorrow. So I curl up under my rock. Then I notice there's another way in. There's a tunnel under the rock and it leads out the other side into a jumble of boulders on the hillside away from the road. Don't know where it leads to but I'm going to find out. If I stay here they'll get me sooner or later.

I'm wriggling along now on my hands and knees. At first I can still hear Mum's voice.

"Stevey," she calls. "Stevey."

I swear she's crying. Then the voice fades out and I'm alone in the tunnel.

It's not exactly a tunnel now. There's a track that winds through boulders that must have fallen down from a cliff somewhere up the hill. At times I've got to crawl under the rocks. In other places I can stand up.

It takes a long time and I've got to stop for a rest. I don't even know if I'll be able to get out the other end.

Then suddenly I am out of it. In front of me there's one of these boggy fields with bracken and broom, and beyond that there are back gardens and houses. I can see now that I've come out just beyond Benderloch village and I'll have to backtrack to get to Fiona's.

I'm crossing the field, running from bush to bush. Now I'll have to cut across the road to get to her house. I look both ways and listen. That police car with Mum could be anywhere. On the other hand they're maybe still back where I left them, still searching. Anyway, the road's clear; so I go up over the fence, sprint down the road and in Fiona's gate. Then I stop. Crouch down behind her hedge. What if her dad's in? It must be about teatime. I glance at my wrist, but my watch isn't there. I must have lost it somewhere with all that scrambling and mud and stuff.

What to do?

I decide to chance it. Got no choice really. I run to the door and ring the bell. I'm sopping wet, but my mouth is dry like dust. What if she's not in?

But she is.

Don't think she recognises me at first – no wonder.

"Hello," I croak. "It's me."

"Steve?"

"Same guy."

"Come in – no, go in the bathroom. Don't mess the place up."

What's she like? After all I've been through.

"Look," she says, "just stay there. I'll get you some dry clothes."

"I've done a runner," I announce dramatically.

"I know." She's pure casual.

"How d'you know?"

"The police checked to see if you were here. Your mum's dead worried."

Then she's off and back again with a bundle of stuff.

"Here's some dry things."

"Girl's clothes?" I wonder, but she's brought a T-shirt, jeans and trainers.

She insists I get washed and changed before she'll listen to my story. Her trainers are too small, so I have to put my own sopping ones back on. But she has to clean all the mud off them first.

I try to explain it's an emergency. I'm on the run, in urgent danger, but she's not for hurrying.

"Listen," she says, "the police have been here already. They won't be back. Dad's library shuts at eight, so he won't be in for a while yet. Just calm down."

When she sees I'm clean and dry (well, almost) she lets me go and sit in the lounge.

Then she's ready to listen, but it turns out she knows most of it already – except the bit about the lift from Darren and Vicki.

It seems that Mum's been phoning around just about everybody trying to find out where I am, and *Radio Oban FM* has just done a newsflash that a boy with red hair has been reported missing in the Dalmally area.

"Right," Fiona says, twirling her ponytail. "I'll have to hide you tonight. Aidan can't be killed till tomorrow. We know exactly where it happens, so we can go into the Land of the Old first thing tomorrow morning and save him. As soon as we come back to today you'll have to go and see your mum. She's back here, you know. She's going to stay here till you're found."

"Let's go to the Land of the Old now and make sure."

"Oh, no." She shakes her head. "Far too risky. We wouldn't have long enough before sunset. Imagine if we met Gawawl in the dark. "Besides," she adds, "I don't want to worry my dad. He'll wonder what's the matter if I'm not here when he gets in. And I've got to make his tea."

Big deal. Aidan's life's on the line and she's worried about her old man's tea! Still, I get it about meeting Gawawl in the dark.

"Now," she says firmly, "you've got to have something to eat and then I'll hide you for the night."

She makes me veggie burger and chips (grilled, not fried) and decaff diet coke. And I'm not allowed tomato sauce because it's not good for you.

When I'm finished I half expect her to tell me to go and brush my teeth, but what she says is, "Downey's barn; that's where you'll sleep."

"Where's that?"

"Downey's is just down the road. He stores hay in it over the winter, but it'll be empty just now. And it's not locked. You'll be all right there."

"What if Downey comes and finds me?"

"No chance. His farm house is on the other side of Ledaig Bay. He never comes here in the summer."

She brings me a rucksack. She stuffs in something like a rolled-up quilt.

"That's a sleeping bag," she tells me. "The barn's got a stone floor. It won't be very comfortable, but you'll be warm enough at this time of year."

We go out her back door to a lane, take a quick look

around and make a dash for it to the side road that leads down to Ledaig Bay.

"The barn's about five minutes' walk from here," she says.

****

The heavy wooden door closes tightly, but there's no lock. It's empty inside – whitewashed walls and a stone floor.

Fiona lays out the sleeping bag.

"What time is it?"

I tell her I've lost my watch.

"Well, it won't be dark for a while yet. So you musn't leave the barn, just in case the police are about. Once it's dark you'll be OK.

"Oh," she adds, "you might hear scuttling noises. These'll be mice, or maybe rats. They won't hurt you. Their whiskers might tickle you when you're sleeping; make you sneeze." She laughs. "Never been camping?"

I'm not exactly over the moon about the rats, but before I've time to worry about them there's something else.

She goes into a side pocket in the rucksack and pulls out the dirk.

"You'd better have this."

"For the rats?"

"Don't be stupid."

"What, then?"

"You remember Gawawl?"

"Do you think I'm gonna forget him?"

"All right. You know that Aidan and Finn and Fergus are only alive in the Land of the Old? They can't be in our today time."

I nod.

"Gawawl and The Morrigan aren't like that. They're immortal."

45

"How d'you mean?"

"They're alive all the time. They never die."

"So?"

"They're in the present as well as the past. They could be with us now."

I freak out. It's like icy spiders are crawling along my spine.

"Don't worry," she goes on. "Remember how your watch strap stopped Gawawl? How do you think he could face a Highland dirk?"

"Will he come after me?"

"Probably not. Whatever he does in the Land of the Old, in today's time he mostly sleeps in the tomb behind your house. So long as nobody disturbs him, that is."

"Then why do I need the dirk?"

"This year's been different because you went into the Land of the Old. I don't know if Gawawl can follow you back into today, and even if he can I don't think he would know where to find you. But take the dirk, just in case."

"Not me. I'm getting out of here."

"Where are you going?" she asks. "Gawawl might just come looking for you but he hasn't a clue that you're in here. Leave this place and it's a toss-up between him and the police."

"I could stay at your place."

Dad would phone the police. He'll be home any minute."

"So it's got to be here?"

"Definitely."

"But if Gawawl doesn't know I'm in here I won't need the dirk."

"Take it just in case. I read somewhere that Gawawl's got an acute sense of smell."

Chapter 9

THE VANISHING
CARAVAN SITE

I'm wakened by a heavy, creaking noise. At first I can't think where I am, but the door opens slowly and a streak of light cuts into the barn.

I remember now, and I think it's Gawawl. I reach for the dirk. But it's only Fiona.

She's brought me tomato sandwiches (wholemeal bread, she says) and a Thermos flask of hot chocolate. Her dad's gone off to his work, so the house is empty, but

Fiona reckons it's too dangerous for me to be seen around Benderloch in today time.

Seems I was on TV last night. *Reporting Scotland* had a bit about me with a photo, and the whole village is out looking for me.

"Everybody's got their eyes skinned." She giggles, "And you're not hard to spot with that red hair."

Mark phoned her up, but she didn't tell him anything. We're not sure about Mark. He might turn me in if he thought it would make him a local hero.

So we decide – well, Fiona's decided already – that we get into the Land of the Old right here in the barn and go to the dead dinosaur in long ago time.

She's been out early picking blaeberries so we can start right away. She produces a polybag full of them. We take half a dozen each, swallow them and squat on the sleeping bag to wait for something to happen.

After about five minutes Fiona asks, "How long did it take last time?"

"Dunno. Can't remember when I picked the berries."

We take another handful, just to be sure.

Another five minutes and I get impatient. "It's not working. You must've got it wrong."

She's angry now. "I didn't get it wrong. It's in MacPhee's book. Anyway, you've not done a lot to try and find out what's going on."

I start to tell her it's me that's done the runner and been chased by the police, but suddenly she snaps her fingers.

"You're dead right. I DID miss something. The book says 'freshly picked.' Perhaps they've got to be absolutely fresh. I got these before breakfast."

"So we'll have to go out and get more."

"Fraid so. I'll go and bring some back," she offers.

"Then they won't be fresh."

"How fresh is fresh?" she asks.

"Maybe you've got to pick them yourself. No point in getting it wrong again."

"All right, but we'll have to be very careful."

I stick the dirk in my belt. That won't help if it's the police that get to me first.

Fiona goes out on to the road. She signals that it's OK and tells me in whispers where to get the berries.

There isn't anybody about, so we could talk normally, but I whisper back, "Let's go for it."

We're on the road that leads past the caravan site with the karting and diving. I hope we get out of today time before we pass it because there's bound to be people about. Fiona leads me off the road into a rocky hollow overgrown with brambles. We pick our way through the thorns, and down among the rocks there's millions of blaeberries.

I only eat two or three, then my cheeks turn inside out. These ones are dead sour.

"Take more," she says.

"How? That's all I had last time."

"That's the point. Last time you came back into today."

"Too right, I did."

"Think about it. We don't want to come back to today till we've completed our mission. So we have to take extra."

Completed our mission! Whew! What's she like?

But I see a problem. "What if we can't get back for days and days?"

"Doesn't matter. Once we've completed our mission we can just hang around till the effect wears off."

"Who's gonna make your dad's tea, then?"

"Don't be sarky."

"OK."

I pick a handful and try to swallow them without chewing. She does the same. The blue juice stains our fingers. I wipe them on my – her – T-shirt. I can see she's not pleased but she doesn't say anything.

"Now what?"

"You tell me. You're the one who's been here before."

"I don't know. I just sort of walked about."

"OK. We'll walk about. But we'll have to watch out for today people who might recognize you."

We go back to the road. We're going to have to pass the caravan site, and I can see there's folk milling about there as usual.

I want to run.

Fiona says, "No. That'll only attract attention."

So we play it cool. We slink along pretending we're dead bored with things. Once we're past the big sign that says:

"GO-KARTING" I want to shout, "Yahoo!" But just then a woman with an English accent shouts, "Hey; that's the kid that was on the box last night. Sonny, come here a moment."

We keep our heads down and walk on.

"Come here," she hollers. "Jeremy, Nigel; catch him."

Two big guys bounce out of somewhere and come after us like Usain Bolt.

"Move," I say.

We leg it.

I'm ahead, but I drop back to push Fiona on. They're faster, but we've a good start and maybe we can dive into bushes and rocks somewhere, like I did when I fooled the police.

We're round a corner now, out of sight for a moment and I'm looking for a place to hide when she trips. She gives a small squawk and she's down in a heap.

I grab her by the elbow and haul her to her feet, but she hasn't got her balance properly and after a couple of steps she's down again.

That's it. Bye-bye Aidan. Back to Paisley for me. I help her up, but there's no hurry now. We're screwed up.

"Keep going," she screams.

"Get real. We're nicked."

"No we're not."

I look back and there's nobody chasing.

"These big guys, where'd they go?" I ask.

Then I see why Fiona tripped. We aren't on the road any more. It's a muddy track full of holes and ruts.

"Have to check this out," I say. "Gotta make sure."

I take her back round the corner to where we ought to be able to see the caravan site. It's not there, only trees and some bracken.

Fiona doesn't seem to realise what's happened, but then she's not done this before, like me.

I tell her, "We've made it to the old land."

"But how?"

"Look." I point. "There should be a sign that says: 'GO-KARTING' – remember?"

She nods.

"Well, where is it?"

"'S not there any more."

"Got it in one."

"OK," she says. "What do we do now?"

"We head for the dead dinosaur."

Chapter 10

THE HILL OF GOLD

We're following the old Bronze Age track. I've not been on this bit of it before, but I'm getting used to finding my way about in the old time. Before long we reach the spot where I met Finn and Aidan and I know it's not far to the dead dinosaur.

It's for real now. I'm trying to remember how I psyched myself the other day – heck, it was only yesterday – to tackle Gawawl.

I tell Fiona, "Not far now."

"You know what to do?"

"Chase Gawawl off with the dirk."

"About the bull, I mean."

I stop. "I thought... "

I don't want to tell her I thought she'd worked all that out.

"How're you going to do it?" she persists.

"You've got the book," I say. "Thought you'd know what it said to do."

"It only said someone of Finn's clan would have to make the sacrifice. So, once you've got rid of Gawawl, you've got to kill the bull."

She wishes! I've just got used to the idea that I could see off Gawawl with the dirk, but slaughtering a bull – I've not even thought about that.

"That's the big one," I say, playing for time. "Gawawl I

can handle." I manage a mini-swagger. "The bull, though...
how to kill a bull... Fergus only killed a goat. Now if it was
just a goat... "

I haven't a clue how to kill a goat, either.

"Or a rabbit?" she snaps.

"A rabbit." I feel a surge of hope. "Would a rabbit do?"

"Sure you could handle a rabbit?"

She doesn't wait for an answer. "Or a mouse?" She's
relentless. "Or a beetle? You could manage to squash a beetle,
couldn't you?"

I don't know where she's at now.

"You idiot. It's got to be the bull. Course you don't have
to do it yourself."

Another surge of hope.

"I'm a McAlpine, too. Want me to do it for you?"

I don't believe I'm hearing this. "You know how to kill a
bull?"

"No."

"Then how... ?"

"Because it's got to be done. Think about Aidan."

She hesitates. "Maybe when the time comes The
Morrigan will make it easy for me."

"Maybe we could let The Morrigan kill it herself."

"You know what the Red Book says."

So do I give the dirk to a bird who's just tripped over her
own feet? Besides, what if she DOES kill it and we go back
to today time and she tells Mark?

I can see the pink gum stuck to his back teeth when he
laughs... "So the bird did the business for you? Big deal."

I've got to bluff this one out.

"OK. I'll sort Gawawl out for you first. Then I'll figure
what to do about the bull."

Hopefully we'll be back into today time before we get
there or the bull will stampede or something.

All this time we're getting closer to the dead dinosaur and suddenly we're round a corner and it's there in front of us with its freshly dug earth and the big stone circle round the base.

Fiona recognises it at once. "There's the way in." She points to the big upright stone slabs.

Then there's that horrible bellowing noise again.

She comes up close beside me.

"Ready with the dirk," she whispers.

I draw it and we enter the tomb.

We're in a long passage with ginormous flat stones at the sides and across the roof. It's dead dark inside, but the sun's shining straight in, so we can see for a bit.

From the other end I can hear bellowing. It thunders among the stones and I'm scared they'll all collapse on top of us. Then I see another light, dim, yellow and flickering, ahead of me.

My hand's sweating on the handle of the dirk.

Fiona squeezes my elbow. "Go on," she whispers.

But I don't. I stop.

We're at the end of the passage. In front of me there's a long, low hall. Round the walls smoky torches are burning; bundles of twigs wedged in cracks in the wall. It's difficult to see cos the light's flickering like strobes at a disco except that it's all the same colour, and the smoke's making my eyes water.

Then the bellowing hits me like an explosion and I see the bull, a big white shape like a ghost, at the other end of the hall. It's got a rope round its neck and it's tied to a post that's stuck in the wall.

"Cut it loose," Fiona hisses. "Get it out of here."

It's an angry bull, as if it knows we're going to try and kill it. It's pawing the ground and snorting, but I think if I can get behind it and cut the rope it'll probably charge straight down the passage and outside.

I push Fiona back into an alcove in the wall in case she gets trampled.

I nip forwards but the bull swings round to face me, so I've got to dodge behind its horns if I'm to cut the rope.

I'm bobbing and weaving like David Haye when there's this shriek behind me:

"Steve."

I spin round and the bull catches me in the ribs with its horn. It's only a glancing blow. Still, it knocks me on the deck. But it can't get far enough to trample me cos it's at the end of its rope.

I look up.

Gawawl's got Fiona. One hairy arm's round her shoulders, pinning her arms. She's thrashing about and kicking. I look right into her eyes and see terror.

His mouth's half open and that slavering tusk's pointing at her throat.

But he doesn't kill her.

He drags her into the alcove – it's much deeper than I'd realised. There's a torch burning at the very back of it and below it there's this huge golden bowl.

Gawawl presses Fiona against it so her neck's on the rim. But he still doesn't kill her.

From somewhere in his skin robes he pulls a knife like the one Fergus used to sacrifice the goat, and places its edge across her throat like a saw.

But still Gawawl does not kill Fiona.

He gazes up somewhere into the flickering darkness under the roof where the light of the torches can't reach and begins to chant, "The Morrigan. The Morrigan. The Morrigan."

I'm like I'm watching a video. It's not real, except that Gawawl's minging and the stench is making my stomach jump up into my throat.

Fiona's gone all still and calm.

"Steve," she says quietly. "The dirk. Go for him. Remember your watch strap."

Her voice is like an explosion in my head. Suddenly I'm real again. I'm in the video. I can change it.

I rush at Gawawl with the dirk out in front of me. I can't remember any of the patter I'd rehearsed the other day. I hear myself shouting "Oh, when the Saints... St Mirren for the cup. Get into these animals."

Just like before, with Aidan, he looks scared. He lets Fiona go, puts up a great hairy paw to hide his face, and steps back into the shadows at the back of the alcove.

She nips round behind me. She's breathing hard.

Gawawl's not done yet. He's cringing, but it seems like he can face cold iron if he looks away. So he comes back for us, roaring and shielding his face with one paw.

"Kill him," demands Fiona.

I remember she's a vegetarian.

But I don't have any choice. He's coming at me with an open mouth and slavering tusks. I know that if I don't get him I'm finished. So I go for it; try to stick the dirk up his nose, just above that gross tooth, but he backs off so quickly that I miss him.

Next thing there's a howl from him, a swirl of skin cloaks and he disappears down a black cave at the back of the alcove.

Fiona says, "He's escaped into the bowels of the earth where we can't follow him."

After we've got our breath back, I ask, "What about the bull?"

"Kill it."

I hand her the dirk. "Not my scene." I don't mind being honest about this now I've seen off Gawawl.

She puts it away with her hand. "Me, neither. I was just winding you up."

"Just have to leave it here, then."

"Can't do that. Gawawl will come out of the earth and get it back. We've got to get it out of here. Go and cut it loose."

This time I'm smarter. I cut the rope before the beast can turn on me and it bolts down the passageway and out into the open.

"Now the cauldron," she says.

Between us we drag it out. It's dead heavy.

"Now what?" I wonder.

The bull's galloped off a bit, but now it's eating grass just like any old cow.

"The Red Book definitely says that it must be sacrificed to The Morrigan," she repeats. "But it's not just that neither of us fancies having to try to kill it. We don't know the proper rituals."

"Rituals? What's that?"

"It's special words you have to say, or maybe things you've got to do. A bit like reciting a magic spell. If you don't get it exactly right it won't work."

That makes me feel a whole lot better. It wasn't that I was too scared to try to kill the bull. No point in trying when it wouldn't have worked anyway. That's the way I'll explain it to Mark.

"Perhaps The Morrigan will find a way to show us," she says.

I laugh.

"Well, she's led us this far safely."

Sometimes Fiona's really spooky.

Chapter 11

THE END OF AIDAN
THE YOUNG

We're just outside the tomb and I'm looking at the bull, wondering how The Morrigan's going to show us how to sacrifice it.

It's not very big, but it's got freaky horns and I don't fancy getting close to it again. I'm thinking *it's quiet enough right now* when suddenly it brings its head up and snorts. It's looking round and listening. I can the whites of its eyes rolling.

Then I hear what it's hearing.

Sort of chiming, like bells, a long way off.

Only I soon realise it's not bells; it's the baying of dogs.

Then there's a crash in the bushes and Aidan bursts out of them with his bronze knife in his hand. He stares around him like a hunted deer. Then he catches sight of me and Fiona.

"The hounds." He waves an arm despairingly.

Four of them break out of a thicket and then check when they see us. They're the biggest, ugliest dogs I've ever seen – black and shaggy – with slavering mouths and lolling tongues.

The three of us get our backs together and they circle us, growling and snarling, as if they are waiting for an order.

Then it comes: "Kill."

The master catches up with them, and it's Fergus with the eye. He checks for a second. Maybe he's surprised to see three kids instead of just one. But he repeats the order: "Kill."

"The dirk," says Fiona quietly.

I know what iron can do, so I'm pure dead gallus. I charge at the dogs, slashing and stabbing left and right and shouting a lot of nonsense. I don't think I hit any of them but they take off in every direction, howling.

Behind me Fergus is cursing his dogs and shouting at them to turn and kill us. I'm not thinking about him, though, until I hear Fiona scream, "Steve."

I spin round and he's coming at me. Aidan slashes at him with his knife and that slows him up just enough for me to show him the dirk.

As soon as he sees it he stops dead, just like Gawawl.

Fergus and me are face to face. Aidan comes up beside me: shoulder to shoulder, his bronze knife and my iron dirk.

For a second Fergus thinks about tackling us. Then I brandish the dirk and he turns and runs.

He doesn't get far. He trips and goes sprawling in the heather. An idea zips across my mind – jump on his back and bury the dirk between his shoulders. Only I don't.

Aidan does! He's on him like a cat, but before he has time to stick him with the blade, Fergus lets out a scream and Aidan bounces off him like he's red hot.

Fergus scrambles to his feet. He's clawing at his throat and I see there's a snake writhing round his neck. It's greenish white with a black zigzag mark down its back, and its teeth are fastened in his throat.

For a moment Fergus staggers about, waving his hands as if he's afraid to touch the thing. Then he pitches forward on to his knees. He's making like he's choking and gurgling now. Then he slumps on to his face and goes quiet.

The three of us freeze. There's a rustling in the heather and I see the black zigzag mark wriggling away.

"The Morrigan," whispers Aidan.

"Fergus is dead." Fiona knows cos it's all in the book. I half expect Aidan to make sure, cut Fergus's throat or something, but he won't even look at the corpse.

So here we are in the middle of the Bronze Age, a dead chief beside us, that wild bull a hundred yards away and all around the invisible presence of The Morrigan.

Fiona's the first to come to her senses.

"Aidan, do you know how to sacrifice the bull?"

He's like he's in a dream.

"My bull," he says. "Born on the same day as I was."

"You must sacrifice it to The Morrigan. You know that."

He shakes his head. "The bull is my brother."

She gets angry with him. "Your father's dead. The dogs would have killed you too. They've killed you before. Aidan, you must."

He sticks his knife in his belt and takes her hand.

"Together we will do the will of The Morrigan."

They're walking towards the bull. I just follow. I'm angry. Fiona said I was the one of the race of Finn who would be the megastar, but then I'm glad I don't have to. Anyway I've got the dirk, so I follow up close just in case things go wrong.

The bull sees us coming and starts bellowing and pawing the ground. Then, I swear, Aidan begins to sing to it.

"Listen summer twilight long
Hearken winter skies afire
Spring and autumn hear my song
Calling all the herds to byre."

He turns to Fiona. "Do you know 'the Great Herdsman of Etive`?"

She nods.

"That's his song."

She joins in. It's like they're charming the animal. It stops snorting and stamping and comes to them like a pet pony.

Aidan scratches its forehead and ruffles its ears as if it's a dog. It nuzzles his hand. He turns to Fiona, "We need the cauldron."

"Steve; the cauldron," she commands.

I'd forgotten all about it, but now I've got to go back for it as if she's The Morrigan herself.

I suppose it's real gold but I'm dragging it behind me, bouncing it off stones, cos it's too heavy to carry. I'm out of breath when I get back to them. "What now?"

"Aidan says we must take the bull and the cauldron across the ford to Eriska, the Holy Island, and he'll show us how to make the sacrifice."

Eriska. It's a long way. I've not been there but Fiona's dad says there's a posh hotel on it in today time and there's a decent road and a bridge today too. But now I've got to drag the cauldron all the way along a bumpy track while they swan along ahead with their pet bull.

"Hey, Fiona. How about taking a shot with the cauldron?"

She half turns and puts her finger to her lips, "Aidan and I are the priest and priestess."

The ford's not deep. Tide's well out. The bull ploughs through with the water round its knees. It's quite sloppy underfoot, though, and I've a bit of a struggle with the cauldron till I realise I can float it across.

In the old time Eriska's a bare moor. Aidan leads the bull to the highest point. There's a big flat stone there and he tells me to put the cauldron on it. I have to wedge it with wee stones to stop it rolling off.

Then he takes his knife and makes Fiona hold it with him, her hand inside his. They're chanting together softly, "The

Morrigan. The Morrigan." The bull's licking Aidan's fingers. Suddenly he makes a quick flick and a jerk and there's blood spurting from a gash in its neck. It lifts its head and moans softly, not that terrible bellowing I heard from the dead dinosaur. More like a sort of sad sigh. Then Aidan and Fiona put in the knife and open up the wound.

The bull's on its knees now, its blood gushing into the cauldron. Aidan's in tears. "My brother," he blubbers. The beast collapses. Aidan's got his arms round its neck and its blood's washing all over him. It gives an enormous shudder. Then it is quite still.

Overhead I hear the raw 'kark` of a raven. For a split second, behind Aidan and Fiona, there flickers the figure of a one eyed hag. Then it's gone. Aidan must have seen it too for he's on his hands and knees, eyes wide and staring.

Fiona crouches beside him and they clasp hands. Then he doubles up like he's been kicked in the stomach. He's trying to hold on to her but, right in front of my eyes, he shrivels and slips like sand through her fingers until there's nothing left but a little pile of dust on the flat stone.

Fiona unclenches her fist. Some fine dust in the lines of her palm blows away in the wind.

The bull's gone, too, and the cauldron that was half full of hot blood is empty with just a rusty stain on the inside.

Fiona's on her knees. Her forehead's on Aidan's dust. She's screaming hysterically, "Aidan. AIDAN. AAAAAI-DAAAAN."

Chapter 12

GAWAWL AGAIN

After a while – quite a long while – Fiona calms down. Then I ask her the big question, "How do we get back?"

"Get back?" She's not with it.

"Yip. Job's done. Bull's sacrificed. Curse is lifted. So how d`we get back to today time?"

"We just do."

"How?"

"You tell me. You've done it twice already."

"That was an accident. I just came out. Like I went in. Don't know how. You PLANNED this one. So how d`we get back?"

"We just wait till the effect wears off."

Then I remember we ate extra berries. "What if it takes days `n' days?"

"What if?"

I've another idea and my heart drops into my stomach at the thought. "Maybe we overdosed. What if we never get back? That book you had said some people never got back."

"I don't know that I want to get back."

I go ballistic. "Not get back! We can't stay here. There's nothing here but monsters. No decent houses... no TV... no football... no..."

She cuts me short. "Don't you care?"

"Care? Course I care. Job's done. Now let's get back."

"Don't you care about Aidan?"

"Aidan? Yes. We saved him from the dogs, like you said. Now he's sorted out, like the bull and Fergus."

"You nerd. You don't care about him. You just think he's a... a..."

"Dead kid from long ago. He's lucky he's dead now. You said he'd be at peace, remember?"

"He was real a moment ago. Now he's dead."

For a moment I think she's going to cry again, but she stays cool.

"Look," she says, "we've got to get it together. Gawawl might be around somewhere."

"And we can't get back to today time."

"Well, that's not my fault."

"You might've thought of a way to do it."

"Why don't you think for yourself sometimes?"

"You've got all the books. Besides, it was you who said to eat extra berries. Never thought it might make us stay here for good, did you?"

I'm really angry with her now. But she just goes quiet.

"I don't care any more."

"No. You just want to curl up and blubber over a dead guy from the Bronze Age."

"You rat. You rotten rat."

I'm sorry I said that, but I don't know how to say I'm sorry. So I change the subject.

"What're we gonna do with this?" I kick the cauldron.

"Doesn't matter."

"Can we take it into today time with us?"

"Why not?" Then she has another thought. "No. We musn't. It's Gawawl's now. We've sacrificed the bull. Gawawl can have the cauldron. It's better that way."

"How?"

"Because if he doesn't get it he'll come looking for it."

"So what? I can handle him." I'm feeling cool again.

Besides, I need a bit of a boost. I'm still sorry at what I said about Aidan. "Come on, Gawawl," I challenge. "I'm waiting."

I'm certain he won't come. It's all over. He's toast, like Aidan and Fergus.

But he's not.

And he does come.

Fiona screams. She can't speak. She's pointing at the ford. The tide's just started to come in. You can see the edge of the water nibbling at the mud on the bank.

There's four or five Firbogs wading across the water up to their knees. Gawawl's in front. I recognise him by that gross tooth. Then the others, red-haired, shaggy, with long arms and enormous chests. Some of them are carrying sticks or stone clubs. I can smell their stink from here.

Fiona finds her voice. "The dirk, Steve."

I reach for it, and my heart drops into my guts. It's gone.

"Quick, Steve." Fiona's still calm.

"It's not there."

"What d'you mean 'not there'?"

"Must've dropped it when we crossed the ford. I'd a job with that cauldron."

"You idiot. You stupid idiot."

"Well you just left me with the cauldron."

"Make it with your watch stra..." her voice tails off. "I'd forgotten you had to lose that, too."

She's clenching and unclenching her fists. "Give them the cauldron. That's what they've come for."

I just stand there.

"Look." She grabs the cauldron and tries to lift it on to its side, but it's too heavy for her. "Help me."

Between us we tip it over on its side.

"Now push," she says.

It rolls off down the hill and picks up speed. It leaps from rock to rock till it hits the water in an explosion of spray. Gawawl tries to grab it, but it's just wide of his reach. At first it floats but it has hit the water side on and starts to fill up. For a moment it swirls round and round. Then it sinks.

The Firbogs flounder over to where it went down. They grope with their long arms and stick their heads under water. Gawawl gets a hold on it and hauls it to the surface. He empties it out and drags it back to the bank, though he doesn't seem to have the sense to float it like I did. He puts it on a rock above high tide and wedges it with a stone so it won't roll off.

Then he turns and stares across the water at us. He waves an arm about and calls his mates round him. Then they start to wade across again.

The tide race is getting faster now, flowing like a river from the sea into the loch. They're still only about knee deep, but suddenly Gawawl stops. He seems to panic. He's floundering about and trying to get out of the water as if it's boiling. They all scramble back to dry land as fast as they can.

I'm wondering – were there crocodiles in Scotland in the Bronze Age?

Back on the mainland the Firbogs gather on the bank. They whoop and scream at us. Gawawl beats the cauldron like a drum. But they won't go anywhere near the water, though it's still quite shallow.

Fiona's got the explanation – as usual: "They can't cross running water. Remember – in MacPhee's book."

We stare them out and after a while they slope off, dragging the cauldron with them.

We sit down on the big flat stone at the top of the island. Fiona says it's holy and we should he safe here. Anyway, Gawawl can't cross the ford till the next low tide and that's tomorrow morning. It's getting dark now, but it's still very warm. She says it was hotter in the Bronze Age; so we won't be cold during the night.

I'm shattered. For a long time I'm too excited to go to sleep but at last I drift off, and I dream that Fiona's on her knees beside me on the big stone and she's chanting softly, "The Morrigan. The Morrigan."

Chapter 13

STILL ALIVE

I wake up chittering.

Whatever Fiona says about the weather in the Bronze Age, it's Baltic now. It must be early morning. There's dew on the grass round us and my clothes are damp.

Fiona's still sleeping.

I look straight down the hill to the ford where Gawawl had to turn back. There's the bridge. Away to the right there's an avenue of trees and a big house; the swish hotel, I suppose.

Then I notice I'm not lying on the holy stone any more. It's just moss and heather.

I give Fiona a shake. "We're back in today."

"Oh."

"Sorry what I said about Aidan."

"That's OK. Where are we?"

"Eriska island."

"Oh, yes."

"So we go home now and I gotta explain to Mum."

Suddenly we're on a different planet.

"Yeah. My dad'll be worried stupid. Steve..."

"Uh-uh."

"Promise me one thing."

"Uh-uh."

"Don't tell Mark."

"What about?"

"You know, Aidan. Don't ever tease me about him, please."

"Better make up a cover story," I suggest.

"How you saved me from Gawawl," she laughs.

"How you sacrificed the bull."

"Better get home." She stands up and dusts herself down. "Your mum was dead worried the other day."

"And your dad."

We trudge across the bridge. Below us the tide is racing in again, with flurries of foam on the crests of little wavelets. *Can evil spirits cross running water by a bridge?* I wonder.

Fiona reads my thoughts: "Not in Tam o' Shanter."

We're on the other side now anyway, but we're in today time; so it doesn't matter. At least I think so.

Fiona has other ideas.

"Look," she says, "there's something we've got to talk about."

"What?"

She twirls her ponytail.

"Member what I told you about Gawawl being immortal? You remember, in Downey's barn, when I gave you the dirk."

"You mean he's in today time too?"

"That's right."

I've had time to think about this since she mentioned it before.

"Why's nobody ever seen him then?"

"Sometimes they have. Remember what MacPhee's book says. A hundred years ago people must've seen him often."

"But not now?"

"Maybe even now. I don't know. There's a lot of local folk, like Mrs. Naysmith, won't walk past Cnoc an Oir after dark. But I do know this: Gawawl keeps the cauldron hidden in there. So long as he's got it – and nobody disturbs him – he sleeps under the hill, at least most of the time."

"So?"

"You musn't tell anybody it's there."

"They'd not believe us anyway."

"Steve, do you know what archaeology is?"

I know the word. "Yes. When we did that project on the Trojan War an archaeologist found the ruins of Troy; so they knew it was true."

"Correct," she says. "Archaeologists dig into tombs and ruins and look for ancient things. What if they thought a golden cauldron from the Bronze Age might be under your dead dinosaur?"

"They'd dig it up."

"Right first time. And Gawawl, he'd waken up and come out to get it back, wouldn't he? Do you want him to waken up in today time?"

I decide the last thing I want is Gawawl on the loose in today time, so I'm not going to tell anybody about the cauldron. But what AM I gonna say to Mum … and Mark? Fiona says it doesn't really matter, so long as we don't breathe a word about the cauldron.

We're coming up to our house now and we agree we'll go in. Then my mum can phone Fiona's dad and let him know she's OK. It's early. There'll be nobody up yet.

At the garden gate we both stop.

"Remember," she whispers, "no cauldron."

I hear myself saying, "Aidan was a king."

She squeezes my elbow.

"By the way," she says in a different voice, "I think your dad'll be here."

Dad! That'll be great. We can go karting at Ledaig tomorrow – after I've had a good sleep.

Mum's at the window. She's not dressed, but she looks like she's been up all night.

She opens the door and rushes out to meet us.

On the ridge of the roof croaks … a raven.